Captain's Purr

MADELEINE FLOYD

HARCOURT, INC.

Orlando   Austin   New York   San Diego   Toronto   London

For Michael, my hero

First published in Great Britain in 2003 by Orion Children's Books,
a division of the Orion Publishing Group Ltd.
First U.S. edition 2003

www.HarcourtBooks.com

Library of Congress Cataloging-in-Publication Data
Floyd, Madeleine
Captain's purr/Madeleine Floyd
p. cm.
Summary: A cat named Captain enjoys a number of activities,
especially spending time with his sweetheart.
[1. Cats–Fiction.] I. Title
PZ7.F66983Cap 2003
[E]–dc21   2002155323
ISBN 0-15-204939-8

A C E G H F D B
Printed in Italy

U.S. edition designed by Scott Piehl
Display lettering created by Judythe Sieck

This is our house by the river where we live.

Here is Captain, our very handsome cat.
We love Captain.

Captain likes to sleep.

He sleeps on my bed.

He sleeps on my books.

He sleeps at the top
of the stairs,

and he sleeps on
the roof of the
garden shed.

When he is not sleeping, Captain likes to wash.

He washes his ears.

He washes his paws.

He washes his back,   and he washes his long tail.

When he is not sleeping or washing, Captain likes to eat.

He eats cat food from small round tins.
He eats cat biscuits from large square boxes.

He eats pink salmon from his special blue plate,
and if he is lucky, he eats little bits of roast chicken
left over from our supper.

When he is not sleeping or washing or eating,

Captain goes out in the moonlight.

He strolls down to the river.

He jumps into his rowing boat.

He picks up the oars, and he rows and he rows

until he reaches the house where his sweetheart lives.

They sit in his boat under the stars,

holding paws and smiling at each other.

Before morning comes,
Captain says good-bye.

Then he rows back up
the river, jumps out of
his rowing boat,

climbs back up the stairs,

strolls back up the garden path,

springs back up onto my bed,
and purrs very loudly.

When Captain is not sleeping or washing or eating or rowing
or holding paws with his sweetheart, he likes to purr.

Captain purrs,
and he purrs,
and he purrs,
and he purrs.